LIBERIA

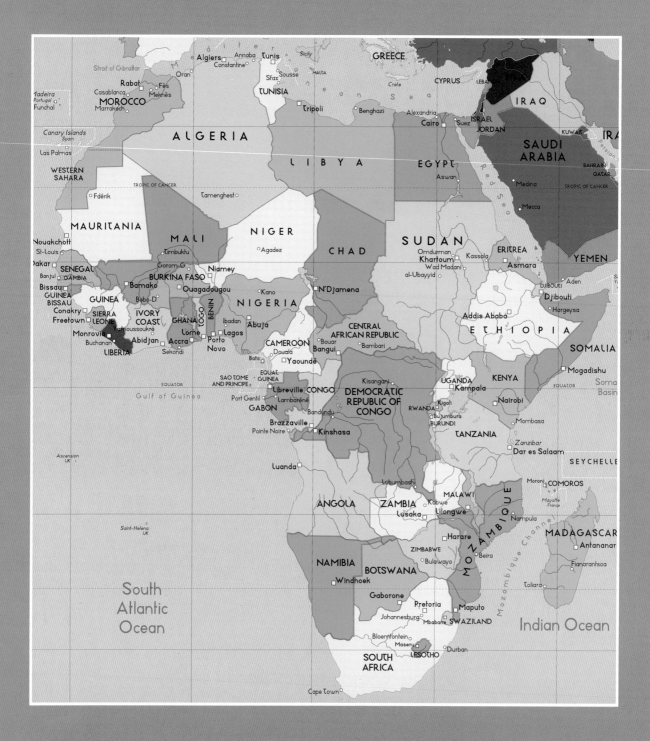

LIBERIA

Brian Baughan

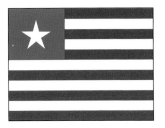

Mason Crest Publishers
Philadelphia

Produced by OTTN Publishing, Stockton, N.J.

Mason Crest Publishers
370 Reed Road
Broomall, PA 19008
www.masoncrest.com

First printing

1 3 5 7 9 8 6 4 2

Library of Congress Cataloging-in-Publication Data

Baughan, Brian.
  Liberia / Brian Baughan.
      p. cm. — (Africa : continent in the balance)
  Includes bibliographical references and index.
  ISBN-13: 978-1-4222-0088-9
  ISBN-10: 1-4222-0088-4
  1. Liberia—Juvenile literature. I. Title. II. Series: Africa (Philadelphia, Pa.)
  DT624.B38 2007
  966.62—dc22

                                      2006017337

Africa: Facts and Figures	**Egypt**	**Nigeria**
The African Union	**Ethiopia**	**Rwanda**
Algeria	**Ghana**	**Senegal**
Angola	**Ivory Coast**	**Sierra Leone**
Botswana	**Kenya**	**South Africa**
Burundi	**Liberia**	**Sudan**
Cameroon	**Libya**	**Tanzania**
Democratic Republic	**Morocco**	**Uganda**
of the Congo	**Mozambique**	**Zimbabwe**

Table of Contents

Africa: Continent in the Balance

Robert I. Rotberg

Africa is the cradle of humankind, but for millennia it was off the familiar, beaten path of global commerce and discovery. Its many peoples therefore developed largely apart from the diffusion of modern knowledge and the spread of technological innovation until the 17th through 19th centuries. With the coming to Africa of the book, the wheel, the hoe, and the modern rifle and cannon, foreigners also brought the vastly destructive transatlantic slave trade, oppression, discrimination, and onerous colonial rule. Emerging from that crucible of European rule, Africans created nationalistic movements and then claimed their numerous national independences in the 1960s. The result is the world's largest continental assembly of new countries.

There are 53 members of the African Union, a regional political grouping, and 48 of those nations lie south of the Sahara. Fifteen of them, including mighty Ethiopia, are landlocked, making international trade and economic growth that much more arduous and expensive. Access to navigable rivers is limited, natural harbors are few, soils are poor and thin, several countries largely consist of miles and miles of sand, and tropical diseases have sapped the strength and productivity of innumerable millions. Being landlocked, having few resources (although countries along Africa's west coast have tapped into deep offshore petroleum and gas reservoirs), and being beset by malaria, tuberculosis, schistosomiasis, AIDS, and many other maladies has kept much of Africa poor for centuries.

Thirty-five of the world's 50 poorest countries are African. Hunger is common. So is rapid deforestation and desertification. Unemployment rates are often over 50 percent, for jobs are few—even in agriculture. Where Africa once was a land of small villages and a few large cities, with almost everyone

Liberia was established on the West African coast during the 19th century as a home for freed slaves.

engaged in growing grain or root crops or grazing cattle, camels, sheep, and goats, today more than half of all the more than 900 million Africans, especially those who live south of the Sahara, reside in towns and cities. Traditional agriculture hardly pays, and a number of countries in Africa—particularly the smaller and more fragile ones—can no longer feed themselves.

There is not one Africa, for the continent is full of contradictions and variety. Of the 750 million people living south of the Sahara, at least 130 million live in Nigeria, 74 million in Ethiopia, 62 million in the Democratic Republic of the Congo, and 44 million in South Africa. By contrast, tiny Djibouti and Equatorial Guinea have fewer than 1 million people each, and prosperous Botswana and Namibia each are under 2.5 million in population. Within some countries, even medium-sized ones like Zambia (11.5 million), there are a

A billboard encourages Liberians to put their country's welfare first.

plethora of distinct ethnic groups speaking separate languages. Zambia, typical with its multitude of competing entities, has 70 such peoples, roughly broken down into four language and cultural zones. Three of those languages jostle with English for primacy.

Given the kaleidoscopic quality of African culture and deep-grained poverty, it is no wonder that Africa has developed economically and politically less rapidly than other regions. Since independence from colonial rule, weak governance has also plagued Africa and contributed significantly to the widespread poverty of its peoples. Only Botswana and offshore Mauritius have been governed democratically without interruption since independence. Both are among Africa's wealthiest countries, too, thanks to the steady application of good governance.

Aside from those two nations, and South Africa, Africa has been a continent of coups since 1960, with massive and oil-rich Nigeria suffering incessant periods of harsh, corrupt, autocratic military rule. Nearly every other country on or around the continent, small and large, has been plagued by similar bouts of instability and dictatorial rule. In the 1970s and 1980s Idi Amin ruled Uganda capriciously and Jean-Bedel Bokassa proclaimed himself emperor of the Central African Republic. Macias Nguema of Equatorial Guinea was another in that same mold. More recently Daniel arap Moi held Kenya in thrall and Robert Mugabe has imposed himself on once-prosperous Zimbabwe. In both of those cases, as in the case of the late Gnassingbe Eyadema in Togo and Mobutu Sese Seko in Congo, these presidents stole wildly and drove entire peoples and their nations into penury. Corruption is common in Africa, and so are weak rule-of-law frameworks, misplaced development, high expenditures on soldiers and low expenditures on health and education, and a widespread (but not universal) refusal on the part of leaders to work well for their followers and citizens.

Conflict between groups within countries has also been common in Africa. More than 15 million Africans have been killed in the civil wars of Africa since 1990, with more than 3 million losing their lives in Congo and more than 2 million in the Sudan. Since 2003, according to the United Nations, more than 200,000 people have been killed in an ethnic-cleansing rampage in Sudan's Darfur region. In 2007, major civil wars and other serious conflicts persisted in Burundi, the Central African Republic, Chad, the Democratic Republic of the Congo, Ivory Coast, Sudan (in addition to the mayhem in Darfur), Uganda, and Zimbabwe.

Despite such dangers, despotism, and decay, Africa is improving. Botswana and Mauritius, now joined by South Africa, Senegal, and Ghana, are beacons of democratic growth and enlightened rule. Uganda and Senegal are taking the lead in combating and reducing the spread of AIDS, and others are following. There are serious signs of the kinds of progressive economic policy changes that might lead to prosperity for more of Africa's peoples. The trajectory in Africa is positive.

Liberia is located in the tropics, and contains a variety of geographic areas. (Opposite) Young boys fish in one of Liberia's many rivers. (Right) An aerial view shows a forested part of Liberia, with a small town visible to the right.

1 A Land of Potential Wealth

LIBERIA, AFRICA'S FIRST INDEPENDENT REPUBLIC, is located in West Africa and is bordered by Sierra Leone, Guinea, the Ivory Coast, and the Atlantic Ocean. Slightly larger in size than the state of Tennessee, this small country is blessed with a tropical climate, abundant mineral deposits, a dense rain forest, and a long coastline—all potential sources of great natural wealth. Unfortunately, in recent decades environmentally unsustainable practices and the ravages of war have prevented Liberians from benefiting from these resources.

Geographic Regions

There are three major geographical areas in Liberia: a coastal region that runs from Sierra Leone in the northwest to the Ivory Coast in the east; a plateau region containing vast expanses of rain forest; and the country's highlands, which straddle the borders of Ivory Coast and Guinea, Liberia's northern neighbor.

The Liberian coastline is low with shallow waters and shifting sandbars. One major geographical obstacle that Liberia once faced was a lack of good natural harbors along its coast, which stretches for 360 miles (579 kilometers). The creation of the country's artificial harbors, which began in the 1940s, eliminated this problem.

The coast's highest *promontory*, Cape Mount in the northwest, rises 1,000 feet (305 meters). There are only two other notable promontories, which are the sites of the port town of Harper at Cape Palmas and the capital city, Monrovia, at Cape Mesurado.

Lagoons and mangrove swamps cover the grasslands and plains of Liberia's coastal region, a strip of land about 25 miles (40 km) wide. Further inland from the coastal plains are rolling hills, which cover an area between 40 and 60 miles (64 and 97 km) wide. The plateau region, located north of the hills, sits at an elevation between 600 and 900 feet (183 and 274 m).

Further north of the plateau are the country's highlands. This region is home to the Nimba mountain range located in the far north and the Wologizi Range in the northwest. The Wologizi Range features Mount Wuteve, Liberia's tallest peak at a height of 4,528 feet (1,380 m). These Liberian ranges form the foothills of the Guinea Highlands.

There are 15 major rivers in Liberia, all of which drain into the Atlantic Ocean. One of these rivers, the Mano, forms the country's northwestern border, while another, the Cavalla, forms the eastern border.

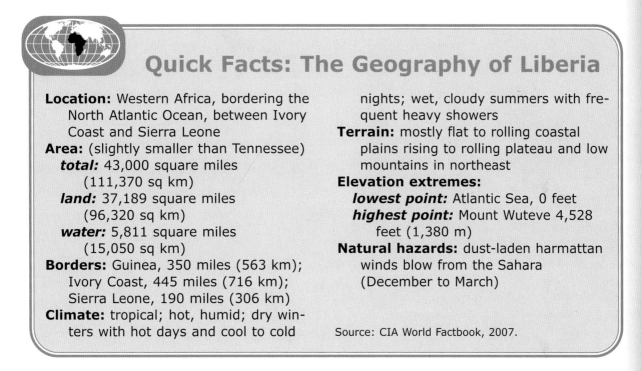

Quick Facts: The Geography of Liberia

Location: Western Africa, bordering the North Atlantic Ocean, between Ivory Coast and Sierra Leone

Area: (slightly smaller than Tennessee)
- *total:* 43,000 square miles (111,370 sq km)
- *land:* 37,189 square miles (96,320 sq km)
- *water:* 5,811 square miles (15,050 sq km)

Borders: Guinea, 350 miles (563 km); Ivory Coast, 445 miles (716 km); Sierra Leone, 190 miles (306 km)

Climate: tropical; hot, humid; dry winters with hot days and cool to cold nights; wet, cloudy summers with frequent heavy showers

Terrain: mostly flat to rolling coastal plains rising to rolling plateau and low mountains in northeast

Elevation extremes:
- *lowest point:* Atlantic Sea, 0 feet
- *highest point:* Mount Wuteve 4,528 feet (1,380 m)

Natural hazards: dust-laden harmattan winds blow from the Sahara (December to March)

Source: CIA World Factbook, 2007.

These and four other major waterways—the Lofa, Cestos, Saint Paul, and Saint John—flow from the mountains of Guinea, while the shorter rivers rise in Liberia's central region. These rivers could comprise an effective transportation network were they easier to navigate, but rapids, narrow channels, and small islands keep vessels from traveling significant distances. The rivers do, however, generate *hydroelectric* energy.

Climate

Liberia has a hot, tropical climate, with an average daily temperature of 80° Fahrenheit (27° Celsius) and continual rains. Next to Buenaventura, Colombia,

A Liberian woman sows rice seeds. Rice is a staple food in Liberia. Unlike many other grains, it can be grown in tropical areas because it is not affected by high moisture.

there is no inhabited place in the world that receives more rain per year than Monrovia, which charts an annual rainfall of 202 inches (513 centimeters). Even the country's driest place, located in the interior, still receives about 70 inches (178 cm) of rain every year.

Liberia only has a rainy season and a dry season. During the rainy season, which begins in April or May and goes through October or November, the coastal plains experience severe flooding. During the dry season, the days remain hot, but the nights are cool. From December to March, the *harmattan* winds that blow from the Sahara Desert bring relief from the humidity but also bring flying dust that hampers peoples' vision.

Most of the country's land can be used for agriculture. The country's soil and hot tropical climate are ideal for growing upland rice, the country's largest food crop, as well as rubber trees, the largest cash crop. Coffee, cocoa, and cassava also grow in abundance, and coconuts thrive in the sandy soil of the coastal zone, along with wild palm trees from which Liberians extract palm oil.

Rain Forest

The Liberian rain forest is a national treasure, covering 31 percent of the country's land area. It makes up 45 percent of the Upper Guinea Forest, which also covers parts of Sierra Leone, Guinea, Ghana, Togo, Guinea-Bissau, the Ivory Coast, and Nigeria. Among the animals that live in the Liberian forest are the Jentink's duiker, the rarest species of sub-Saharan antelope in the world. The rainforest is also home to pigmy hippopotamuses, monkeys, mongoose, chimpanzees, leopards, cats, and hundreds of species of birds, nine of which are endangered. Many plants with medicinal qualities have been found among the 2,000 or so different types of flowering plants that *ecologists* have identified in the rain forest.

However, in recent years unsustainable practices have threatened the forest's diverse plant and animal life. In past years, particularly during the 14-year-long civil war that ended in 2003, timber companies ignored logging regulations, and the court system failed to take legal action against them. the Save My Future Foundation estimates that log production increased by more than 1,300 percent between 1997 and 2001, and that logging and other unsustainable practices in West Africa have reduced the Upper Guinea Forest from an area of 281,043 square miles (727,900 sq km) to only 35,829 square miles (92,797 sq km)—12.7 percent of its original size.

In response to these logging *infractions*, the United Nations imposed *sanctions* on Liberian timber exports in 2003. The transitional government that was formed that year failed to meet the conditions to lift the *embargo*, and as a result the sanctions were renewed in 2004 and again in 2005.

Liberia was devastated by a 14-year-long civil war, marked by many atrocities. (Opposite) A masked member of warlord Charles Taylor's armed militia walks past the body of a dead enemy in Monrovia, August 1990. (Right) Refugees flee from the capital as rebel forces attempt to capture the city, July 2003.

2 Struggling for Liberty

THE NAME "LIBERIA," coined nearly two centuries ago, refers to the liberty that white American colonizers wished freed slaves would find in their new African settlement. Although it is true that the few thousand slaves who were transplanted to the West African coast gained freedoms that were previously denied them by their American masters, the same could not be said for the majority of the country's *indigenous* peoples, the original residents who came be to be oppressed by the Americo-Liberian elite.

Liberian leaders eventually righted some of the wrongs done to the country's native people by giving them more of a say in government. However, during the 20th and 21st centuries a number of other problems continued to plague the country, including extreme poverty, corruption, and political repression. Today most Westerners know Liberia for the long and

17

brutal civil war that raged from 1989 to 2003. During these years rival armies—many composed of children—committed horrific crimes against fellow citizens and other West Africans. All the while, the country's economy collapsed and the *infrastructure* nearly fell apart.

The Original Settlers

Although the accounts are far from complete, a historical record does exist of Liberia before it became an independent republic. Historian John-Peter Pham estimates that there were between 100,000 and 150,000 people living in the region before the white settlers and freed slaves arrived in 1820. They consisted of three main groups: the Kwa-speaking, Mel-speaking, and Mande-speaking peoples.

The Kwa-speaking peoples, who are subdivided into the Krahn, Kru, Bassa, and Grebo ethnic groups, are believed to have begun migrating from the north and the east during the 13th century. The Mel-speaking peoples, subdivided into the Gola and Kissi, arrived around 1300 or 1400. These groups were originally subjects of the Western Sudanic empires occupying regions to the north. In 1455 the entrance of the Mande-speaking peoples from Mali, who specialized in trade, marked a major change in the region's settlement. This new group pushed the Mel and the Kwa southward, a trend that continued as more Mande arrived over succeeding years.

While these three groups were establishing themselves in the region, European nations were expanding their *maritime* trade. Portuguese seafarers and traders arrived in the land that would become Liberia in 1461 and were soon followed by the British and the Dutch.

The Portuguese are responsible for many of Liberia's present-day place names, including Cape Mesurado and the Grain Coast. Their name for the Liberian coast derived from the popular melegueta pepper, whose seeds were known as "grains of paradise." In addition to peppers and other spices, which could be sold in Europe at a great profit, the Portuguese also traded for handwoven cotton cloth, ivory, gold, and palm oil. However, they were most interested in purchasing slaves, as the West African slave trade was highly profitable for all involved. The Mandingo and other Mande-speaking tribes were the most prominent trade partners with the Portuguese, having acquired slaves during wars with other tribes, while the Kru, a Kwa-speaking group of seafarers that had settled on the coast, helped foreign sailors navigate the local waters.

Returning to the Homeland

In the early 19th century, the West African coast offered a solution to a problem that Americans faced at the time: what should be done with freed slaves—those who had escaped their bonds but had little chance of settling comfortably in a country where slavery was still legal in many states? The members of the American Colonization Society (ACS) believed the proper solution was to return the freed slaves to Africa.

The ACS first convened on December 21, 1816. The diverse membership of the organization—composed of northerners and southerners, *abolitionists* and plantation owners—reflected its mixed agenda. For abolitionists the group existed to help former slaves; slaveholders wished to expel freed blacks from the United States so they could not stir up violent revolts among

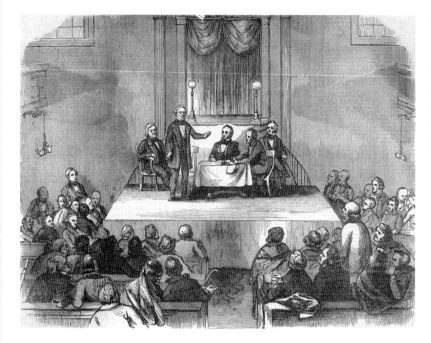

This illustration depicts a meeting of the American Colonization Society in Washington, D.C. The organization was formed in the early 19th century to help return freed blacks to Africa.

those still enslaved. (Proponents of this latter view typically bolstered their argument by citing the Haitian slave rebellion of 1791, in which slaves living in the Caribbean island nation had successfully revolted against their French oppressors.) In one of his letters ACS founder Reverend Robert Finley stated the organization's different leanings in the same sentence: in addition to offering the blacks "a better situation," he wrote, the resettlement option also promised that America "should be cleared of them."

The ACS faced several setbacks in trying to colonize the West African coast. Of the 86 settlers and three officials who arrived in 1820, 22 settlers and all three officials died of yellow fever or malaria. The two diseases would continue to take their toll. According to John-Peter Pham in *Liberia: Portrait of a Failed State*, half of all the settlers lost their lives to poor health over just a few decades. After a second failed attempt to plant a colony, ACS agents made it to Cape Palmas in 1821, eager to negotiate for land with the Dei and Bassa chiefs. The proceedings were far from friendly (the boat's captain put a gun to the head of one of the chiefs), but in a feeble attempt at fairness the settlers offered the leaders "six muskets, one barrel of gun powder, six iron bars, one barrel of rum," and a random assortment of other items in exchange for territory to establish their colony. This agreement constituted the original land claim for what became the colony of Monrovia. The Maryland State Colonization Society, an affiliate group of the ACS, founded a second colony in 1831 in the southeast region near Cape Palmas, which came to be called Maryland County.

The lack of legitimacy was a pressing issue facing Monrovia. Because it had not acquired a U.S. charter signed by Congress, it was not treated like an official colony. Even after it became the Commonwealth of Liberia in 1839, the United States refused to acknowledge the settlers' *sovereignty*. Subsequently, whenever Liberia had a dispute with a European power like Great Britain or France, which by that time had colonized the neighboring lands today known respectively as Sierra Leone and Ivory Coast, the smaller colony could not draw on U.S. resources to press its claims.

By the mid-1840s the ACS had grown weary of its obligation to Liberia and called on the commonwealth to sever its ties and declare independence. In 1847, 12 delegates signed a formal declaration containing language that was inspired by the U.S. Declaration of Independence. Similarly, the Liberian constitution, ratified that same year, established a government modeled on the U.S. government, with a three-part system consisting of a judicial branch, a *bicameral* legislature, and an executive branch headed by a president.

Unfortunately, Liberia also followed the United States's lead in denying basic rights and citizenship to large segments of the population. Just as blacks and Native Americans were excluded in the United States, Liberia's constitution denied native Africans the right to own property, without which they could not vote. Countless conflicts resulted from this legal division between an Americo-Liberian elite that lived along the coast and a native population that was basically relegated to the interior.

Under the leadership of its first president, Joseph Jenkins Roberts (1809–76), Liberia tried to obtain official recognition as an independent state. Great Britain, which believed Liberia could act as an effective partner in its campaign to end the international slave trade, was the first to establish official relations. It was followed by France and, finally, the United States.

Pacifying the Interior

During the republic's early years, the government worked to pacify the people of the interior. In the Sinoe War, which broke out in 1855, Kru living near Greenville lashed out against a trade embargo that President Roberts had issued against them. After the Kru attacked the settlement at Greenville harbor, the government retaliated harshly, and the natives suffered heavy casualties and the *dispossession* of their land.

In 1857 the colony of Maryland County asked Liberia for assistance in dealing with their own Kru uprising. Liberia sent troops to help the

Marylanders, and after the uprising was put down, Maryland County joined the Republic of Liberia.

The Grebo, a confederation of Kwa-speaking tribes living in the Cape Palmas region, had better success contending with the government during the 1870s. Their demands—to win back land stolen from them and gain citizenship—were hard to dismiss on solid grounds. The Grebo declared their region independent from Liberia and began trading freely with foreign ships. Liberian government forces moved against the Grebo by invading their garrison in October 1875, but they were beaten back. By the following year, the Grebo had control of all of Maryland County except for the coastal town of Harper. In exchange for acknowledging the authority of the government in Monrovia, the Grebo were granted full citizenship.

As various European powers seeking to solidify control of African lands encroached on Liberia's borders, it became imperative for

Joseph Jenkins Roberts—known as the "father of Liberia"—was born in Virginia in 1809 and moved to Liberia in 1829. Roberts became governor of Liberia in 1841, and helped Liberia win its independence in 1847. Roberts was the country's first president, serving in that post until 1856. He also served a later term as president from 1872 until his death in 1876. This photograph was taken around 1851.

the Monrovian administration to assert control over the interior. At the Berlin Conference of 1884–85, which was attended by representatives of the United

States, the Ottoman Empire, and many European countries, the doctrine of "effective occupation" was among the emerging policies that would affect Liberia. This doctrine stated that if a government failed to assert control over its indigenous peoples, their lands belonged to the colonial power that could subdue them.

Liberia, still lacking U.S. protection, was struggling to meet the standard of effective occupation in the places where Britain and France were ready and able to establish control. Liberian president Hilary Johnson had ordered the opening of the port at Cavalla near Harper in 1885, which was strongly resisted by the Kru in the territory. Because Liberia was unable to control the natives, France believed it was justified in extending the western borders of its protectorate that would become the Ivory Coast, claiming land beyond the San Pedro River as far west as the Cavalla River. In 1892 France forced negotiations with Liberia. In exchange for handing over all territory east of the Cavalla, Liberia received 25,000 francs and was granted sovereignty west of the river. Forced to also negotiate with Britain, Liberia agreed to sign the Anglo-Liberian Boundary Treaty, which established its western border with Sierra Leone at the Mano River.

A photograph of huts built by the Gola people in western Liberia, circa 1900. Native dwellings like these were subject to taxation by the government.

For a long time, the Liberian government lacked a proper administrative structure for the interior, but one was finally established in 1904. An arrangement known as the Barclay Plan, named after then-president Arthur Barclay, divided the existing territories into districts along ethnic lines. The district borders were often arbitrarily drawn, as the ethnic groups were not always easily defined or settled in a specific area. However, the new setup enabled the Liberian administration to govern the interior and the rest of the country through a new *hierarchy* made up of district chiefs. Although these leaders continued to be selected through traditional customs, their appointments were ultimately subject to the approval of the government.

The new system came with a number of repressive measures, including a "hut tax" that was assessed on native dwellings. (The government, still made up of the Americo-Liberian elite, retained the power to determine what constituted a "native dwelling.") This system remained basically unaltered until the Americo-Liberian leadership was removed from government in 1980.

An Industry Is Born

The United States and the countries of Europe recognized Liberia's natural wealth, particularly the mineral resources found in the northern regions and along the Mano River. However, the country lacked the infrastructure—the roads, bridges, and railways—that would make mining and other operations efficient. At the turn of the 20th century, a British firm invested in this infrastructure in exchange for the right to extract Liberia's resources. It also issued a large loan to Liberia, but over the next few years poor financial management resulted in the government failing to meet its loan payments. Subsequently, the country's foreign debt continued to rise.

To help resolve the growing debt, in 1912 American bankers partnered with European lenders to issue Liberia a sizable loan. But in the years that followed, the Liberian government failed to meet its financial goals, and requests for additional loans were denied. With the state teetering on economic collapse, a new solution arose in the form of a landmark deal to produce rubber in Liberia.

During the early 20th century, the growth of the automobile industry was spurring demand in rubber, and it was clear that rubber trees would thrive in Liberia's hot and humid climate. The American company Firestone, which was looking to break up a British monopoly on rubber production, agreed to a very affordable lease of one million acres (4,047 sq km) of land about 30 miles (48 km) east of Monrovia. The deal was undoubtedly a much greater boon to the investors than to the plantation workers, but the arrangement did help initiate development of the country's infrastructure, which at that point was virtually nonexistent.

The arrangement also helped Liberia avert a financial crisis, although depressed rubber prices during the worldwide depression of the 1930s resulted in limited production. A much-needed boom occurred during World War II (1939–45), when the U.S. demand for natural rubber soared. Liberia became the Allies' main supplier of rubber. The United States also identified the Liberian coast as a strategic place to refuel and maintain aircraft, and the Defense Areas Agreement of 1942 authorized the construction of U.S. military installations. A year later, the United States repaid Liberia the favor by

The American rubber company Firestone invested in Liberia during the 1930s. Firestone remains a major employer, operating a plantation that contains approximately 8 million rubber trees.

signing the Mutual Aid Agreement, which authorized the construction of Liberia's first artificial deepwater port in Monrovia.

Under the leadership of President William V. S. Tubman, elected in 1944, the Liberian economy was revitalized. His Open Door Policy, which invited the country's trade partners to invest in the Liberian economy and enjoy tax benefits, coincided with the completion of the Monrovia port in 1948. By 1952 Liberia had paid off its foreign debt and was enjoying a rare moment of financial independence.

Tubman's early years also were highlighted by the Unification Policy, which threatened the power of the America-Liberian elite by extending the vote to women and indigenous people and offering government positions to native Liberians. However, although indigenous groups could vote, they could not register new political parties, and several police organizations that formed under Tubman kept any resistance in check. Members of the opposition were sent a clear message when Samuel Daniel Coleman, chairman of the Independent Whigs, was killed in 1955. With the power of the dominant True Whig Party unchallenged, Liberia remained a *one-party state*. By changing the constitution's limit on presidential terms, Tubman was able to stay in office for seven straight terms.

Tubman's long presidency ended with his death in 1971. His more tolerant successor, Vice-President William R. Tolbert Jr., inherited a soaring national debt that he could not curb. The economy was particularly hit by changes in world market prices, and with the population lacking basic necessities like clean water, domestic production slowed. In 1979 Tolbert proposed to raise the price of imported rice as a way to force an increase in production of this staple crop. The unpopular solution was met with violent demonstrations that became known as the Rice Riots. Capitalizing on the people's outrage at the president, a master sergeant and ethnic Krahn named Samuel Doe began planning a coup.

Failed Redemption

Few leaders were spared when Doe's 1980 coup succeeded in overthrowing the Tolbert administration. Members of Doe's People's Redemption Council

(PRC) stormed into the executive mansion, killing Tolbert and 26 government leaders. Shortly after, 13 cabinet members were publicly executed.

As Liberia's first indigenous leader, Doe seemed an answer to the prayers of Liberia's long-oppressed majority. His administration made gestures at democracy, forming a National Constitutional Commission that ratified a new constitution in 1986. However, in reality Doe was a ruthless *despot*, given to abusing his people through torture, false arrests, and

Liberian President Samuel K. Doe (left) is surrounded by military personnel during a 1982 visit to the United States. Doe came to power in a 1980 military coup, becoming the first person of African descent to rule Liberia. However, he soon proved to be a ruthless dictator who favored a few ethnic groups over the rest of his country's citizens.

biased trials. To stay in power, he rigged the vote to win the 1985 presidential election.

Rebel leader Charles Taylor brandishes an AK-47, May 1990. Taylor's National Patriotic Front of Liberia was formed to overthrow Doe's government.

Most indigenous Liberians did not attain the equal standing with the Americo-Liberians they had hoped for following Tolbert's overthrow. Instead of smoothing the playing field, the Doe administration replaced the favoritism that had been shown toward the settler elite with preferences for the Krahns and, to a lesser extent, the Mandingo. Doe was afraid of losing his power, so he excluded all other ethnic groups from politics. When Brigadier General Thomas Quiwonkpa attempted a coup in 1985, the president sent his Krahn brigades to brutally murder Quiwonkpa and 3,000 Gio and Mano residents of Quiwonkpa's homeland in Nimba County.

As brutal as his tactics were, Doe failed to preserve his power base for long. By 1989 Charles Taylor, a former minister of commerce, had assembled a small group of rebel soldiers in the Ivory Coast. On Christmas Eve of that year, Taylor invaded with his small group of 168 exiles known as the National Patriotic Front of Liberia (NPFL) with plans to overthrow Doe. Upon crossing the Liberian border, they were joined by thousands of Gio and Mano fighters.

Doe failed to meet his enemies head-on, and his attacks on villagers only shifted popular opinion toward the side of the NPFL. By May 1990 the NPFL had won several battles against the government army, the Armed Forces of Liberia (AFL), and captured the port town of Buchanan and the city of Gbarnga, where Taylor set up a *provisional* capital.

The NPFL eventually grew to outnumber government forces through a style of recruitment for which Taylor became infamous. The NPFL conscripted orphaned children, some as young as eight, to form Taylor's Small Boy Units. Preyed upon at such impressionable age, these children could be counted on for their loyalty. They would eagerly carry out orders to commit murder and other savage acts on villagers, instilling a general fear of the NPFL.

The Conflict Intensifies

By August 1990 the conflict had escalated into a civil war that had already claimed 5,000 lives and made 345,000 Liberians refugees. That month the Economic Community of West African States (ECOWAS), a group committed to economic cooperation in the region, convened in Banjul, the capital of Gambia, to figure out a way to bring peace to Liberia. Leaders at the meeting commissioned the ECOWAS Cease-fire Monitoring Group (ECOMOG), a peacemaking force made up of 3,000 soldiers from seven countries, and appointed Amos Sawyer as president of the transitional government they planned to help set up following Doe's removal.

Both the Organization of African Unity and the United Nations approved the Banjul resolutions. Taylor and the NPFL did not, which meant that the country would remain divided. Taylor declared himself the president of Greater Liberia, a region that he hoped to create by extending the country's borders into Sierra Leone.

With both ECOMOG and the NPFL moving closer toward removing the president, Doe's days were numbered. Ironically, neither of these forces administered the fatal blow. Instead, an NPFL splinter group known as the Independent National Patriotic Front of Liberia (INPFL) stormed the Executive Mansion in September 1990. These rebels captured Doe, tortured him, and dragged him through the streets to be publicly humiliated as he bled to death.

INPFL leader Prince Yormie Johnson immediately dubbed himself president. Although ECOMOG quickly removed Johnson from power and sent him into exile in Nigeria, it was clear that ECOMOG had little control over the combatants, which at one point consisted of seven major groups.

As the war intensified, ECOMOG shifted from its original focus on peacemaking to participating as combatants. Following Doe's assassination, ECOMOG launched a strong offensive against the NPFL, now entrenched in the eastern section of Monrovia. The attack was so effective that it forced the NPFL to agree to a ceasefire in November 1990. However, although Taylor attended power-sharing discussions in February 1991, he refused to agree to terms. Over the next six years, there would be several more peace agreements. Each one was derailed by Taylor.

Economic and social life in Liberia disintegrated during the fighting. Faction leaders funded their military operations by encouraging their foot soldiers to loot citizens and hijack the country's sources of revenue. There were allegations that even ECOMOG troops participated in the looting and harassment of civilians. However, the NPFL remained the most ruthless of the combatants and the most effective at securing revenue from the country's timber, iron ore, gold, diamond, and rubber operations.

Looking to further expand its revenue, the NPFL next turned to the many diamond mines of Sierra Leone. It helped the Revolutionary United Front (RUF), a Sierra Leonean rebel group, launch its rebellion in March 1991 on the Liberia-Sierra Leone border. In exchange for the NPFL's guns, the RUF supplied diamonds that it secured by terrorizing civilians through a brutal campaign of rape and amputation. These became known as "blood diamonds."

International Intervention

It seemed that the only realistic solution to the crisis depended on international mediation. This finally began in November 1992 when the United Nations enacted an arms embargo to cut off some of the supplies to NPFL. Next, the United Nations Observer Mission in Liberia (UNMIL) was formed to enforce the Cotonou Peace Agreement of July 1993, which scheduled a ceasefire to begin the following month and made plans to form a transitional government. Working in coordination with a contingent of peacekeeping troops from the Organization of African Unity, UNMIL worked to disarm the population and maintain peace in embattled regions.

The disarmament process was slow. The Liberian National Transition Government, set up in March 1994, was marred by internal rivalry, and its control never extended beyond Monrovia. Following more failed treaties and

ECOMOG peacekeeping troops from Mali walk off a large transport plane at Liberia's Roberts International Airport, February 1997. The peacekeeping force was sent to Liberia to enforce the Abuja Accord and end the civil war.

a long battle in Monrovia in April 1996 that claimed 5,000 lives, a peace accord signed in Abuja, Nigeria, finally established an effective plan for disarmament and scheduled an election for May 1997. This time, peacemakers were empowered to place sanctions on factions if the accord was broken.

In the end the nine-year civil war resulted in the deaths of over 150,000 people and the internal displacement of another 800,000. An additional 700,000 Liberians fled to neighboring countries. Liberia was in ruins, and the people wanted peace at any cost, even if it meant having Charles Taylor as president. As the one individual who determined whether fighting would continue in Liberia, he had secured the reluctant support of the majority of people in the months leading up to the presidential election. Many voted for Taylor, hoping his election would end the fighting. Taylor won over 75 percent of the vote and took office in August 1997.

A Short Peace

As many expected, Liberia did not find stability under Taylor. He suppressed virtually any form of dissent, filled the Liberian army with his own NPFL comrades, and instead of rebuilding the war-torn economy, sent it further into decline. Taylor's administration was rife with corruption.

Desperate to be rid of President Taylor for good, a rebel army called Liberians United for Reconciliation and Democracy (LURD) emerged in 1999, launching a revolt that dragged the country into war once again. LURD would ravage the countryside for the next several years in its campaign against Taylor's anti-terrorism units.

During this time, Liberia continued to face accusations from the rest of the world of continuing to support the RUF and its "blood diamond" trade. In 2000 the United Nations issued an embargo on the import of diamonds from Liberia, in addition to a new arms embargo and a travel ban on any senior government member who provided support to rebel movements in neighboring countries.

By early 2003 Taylor's government, suffering from effects of the international isolation, was unable to defend itself against two rebel campaigns—the LURD onslaught in the north and the Movement for Democracy in Liberia (MODEL) revolt in the south. The total numbers of casualties were massive— the Liberian death count since 1989 had grown to more than 200,000—and

Supporters of LURD leader Sekou Damateh Conneh rally during Liberia's presidential campaign in September 2005. In 1999 LURD launched an insurrection that helped force Charles Taylor into exile four years later.

world leaders began demanding Taylor's immediate resignation. He finally consented to leave his position in exchange for receiving safe harbor in Nigeria, where he could avoid arrest by the Special Court of Sierra Leone, a tribunal that had indicted him on 17 counts of war crimes and crimes against humanity.

U.S. and United Nations peacemakers supervised the transfer of power in August 2003. During that same month a new interim government signed a peace agreement with rebel forces in Accra, Ghana. The transitional government appointed Gyude Bryant as chairman, a position he held for two years while preparing the country for new elections.

In the November 2005 presidential election, Harvard-educated finance minister Ellen Johnson-Sirleaf beat George Weah, a professional soccer player-turned-politician, to become Liberia's new president. Inaugurated in January 2006, Johnson-Sirleaf recognized the difficult challenges ahead of her in leading the country's reconstruction, although the new government could take encouragement in the progress of the disarmament program: according to an October 2005 Human Rights Watch report, more than 101,000 combatants—11,000 of them children—had already handed in their weapons.

Charles Taylor remained in Nigeria until 2006, when Johnson-Sirleaf officially requested his extradition. In June 2006 Taylor was sent to The Hague to be tried by the Special Court for Sierra Leone for crimes committed in that country's civil war.

After decades of war and repression, in 2006 democracy returned to Liberia. (Opposite) A Liberian man casts his ballot in Monrovia, October 2005. (Opposite) Ellen Johnson-Sirleaf is sworn in as Liberia's president on January 16, 2006. She became the first woman elected to lead an African state.

3 Extending Democracy

WHEN LIBERIA BECAME Africa's first republic in 1847, its founding fathers intended the country to have a democratic government—at least for the Americo-Liberian elite. For much of the country's history, the native Liberian majority was excluded from the political process. Liberia has seen significant changes in recent decades, however. The end of the 20th century marked the beginning of a form of government that better reflected the desires of indigenous people, while the beginning of the 21st marked the return of accountable leadership.

After her inauguration in January 2006, President Ellen Johnson-Sirleaf took on the burden of leading a reconstituted government and restoring the country's faith in its leaders. Between the peace accord of 2003 and the election of Johnson-Sirleaf, most of the cabinet positions and the legislative seats of the Liberian parliament were shared by members of the warring parties—the National Patriotic Party (the former ruling organization), the LURD party, and the MODEL party. The 2005 parliamentary election, which coincided with the presidential election, ushered in a new legislature.

The Three Branches

Liberia's original constitution, which was revised in the mid-1980s, drew heavily on the U.S. Constitution; in fact, the author of the document's first draft was a Harvard University professor. Thus the framework for Liberia's government shares with the United States a strong central leadership, popular elections, an independent *judiciary*, and a balance of powers between three government branches—the executive, judicial, and legislative.

Like the U.S. president, the head of Liberia's executive branch enjoys the power to appoint many important government officials. All appointments, however, are subject to the consent of both houses in the legislature. The president selects ambassadors, justices of the Supreme Court, the superintendents who govern Liberia's 15 counties, and 21 cabinet ministers who oversee government departments like agriculture, finance, justice, and health and social welfare.

The president shares leadership with a vice president, who presides over the Senate in addition to his or her other functions. The vice president is elected on the same ticket with the president, and both leaders can serve a maximum of two six-year terms in office.

Liberia's judicial branch, like the U.S. judiciary, enforces the laws of the country. It is headed by the Supreme Court, which is led by a chief justice and four associate justices. These officials are appointed by the president with the approval of the Senate. They retire at the age of 70, and the only other way they may leave their position is if they are impeached.

Below the Supreme Court are criminal courts, an appeals court, and, in the counties, magistrate courts. Within the tribal communities of Liberia (known as chiefdoms), there are also traditional courts, which administer justice according to a legal code based on tribal law. In these chiefdoms, which are typically governed by leaders called paramount chiefs, tribal law takes precedence in a number of situations, including family law, disputes over land use, and matters of inheritance.

The legislature, made up of a Senate and House of Representatives, is responsible for managing the country's finances, approving treaties and other international agreements, regulating trade, and creating new laws. A bill becomes a law by going through both houses. As in the United States, the Liberian president has veto power over a bill, but that veto can be overridden by a vote of a two-thirds majority in each house.

The legislative elections of 2005 filled the 30 seats of the Senate and the 64 seats of the House of Representatives. Two senators hail from each of the counties, and there are at least two representatives per county with the possibility of more depending on the number of registered voters in the country. Half of the leaders in the Senate are senior senators and serve nine-year terms while the other half are junior senators who serve for six-year periods. Representatives also serve six-year terms.

Before Charles Taylor's resignation, his National Patriotic Party (NPP) was the ruling party, holding 71 total legislative seats out of the 90 seats then available in the House and Senate. In the 2005 elections, several parties competed to fill the positions left by the NPP, which had largely fallen out of favor. Leading the opposition was the Congress for Democratic Change (CDC), the party of presidential challenger George Weah. The CDC, which championed the decentralization of government and the end of government corruption, claimed 15 seats in the House of Representatives and 3 in the Senate. The Coalition for the Transformation of Liberia (COTOL) placed just behind the CDC in the legislative race, winning seven Senate seats and eight in the House of Representatives. A coalition of four separate parties, COTOL was led by presidential candidate Varney Sherman, an educational reform advocate. President Johnson's Unity Party won only 11 seats—8 in the House and 3 in the Senate.

Dealing with the Issues

Liberia's founding fathers established a divide between the elite and the rest of the country that is still not completely bridged today. The revisions in the 1986

A campaign sign for George Weah, the candidate of the Congress for Democratic Change in the 2005 presidential election. Although Weah did not win, his party did gain the largest block of seats in Liberia's legislature.

constitution made modest gains by including all the country's ethnic groups in the political process, but many believe the Americo-Liberians still hold power at the expense of the people of the interior.

An important article of the 1986 constitution stated that political parties could be organized along ethnic, religious, or other lines. Many feared that opening up the political arena in this manner would create conditions that would allow one group to dominate others. As a preventive measure, the writers of the new constitution included a requirement that political parties must have a minimum of 500 members in each of at least six counties. This quota helped ensure that political agendas more closely represented a national consensus than the views of a particular ethnic or regional group.

Many Liberians believe there are other political obstacles standing in the way of indigenous groups, including the manner in which county superintendents enter their positions. If superintendents gained office through popular election rather than presidential appointment, opponents argue, they would more closely reflect the positions of county residents. These leaders advocate for the passage of a constitutional amendment that would remove this special appointing power from the president.

As more and more indigenous groups participate in the political process, some people wonder if the next step is to extend the vote to the country's foreign-born population. The constitution currently excludes those who are not black from voting, as well as from acquiring citizenship or owning property. Some 4,000 Lebanese, Indians, and whites currently live in the country. These foreigners hope the constitution can be expanded so that all residents can participate in the country's ongoing reforms.

Liberia's economy is slowly recovering from the decades of civil war. (Opposite) A cargo ship prepares to unload goods in Monrovia. (Right) Workers empty sacks of freshly tapped rubber, one of the country's most important exports.

4 A Recovering Economy

EVEN BEFORE THE FIRST SHOTS of their civil war were fired, many Liberians were familiar with extreme poverty. The country's export-driven economy had long been vulnerable to the changes in international prices for rubber, timber, iron ore, and diamonds. During the civil war, already weak industries crumbled, and warlords hoarded the country's scarce resources, leaving the average Liberian to scramble for basic necessities. Such desperate conditions helped earn the country the label "the world's worst place to live" in 2003.

The national economy suffered immediate setbacks from the fighting. Economist.com reported that a year into the civil war, domestic production had been reduced by more than four-fifths. The financial numbers recorded by the end of the war were equally alarming. The ***gross domestic product (GDP)***

Quick Facts: The Economy of Liberia

Gross domestic product (GDP*): $2.911 billion

Inflation: 15% (2003 est.)

Natural resources: iron ore, timber, diamonds, gold, hydropower

Agriculture (76.9% of GDP): rubber, coffee, cocoa, rice, cassava (tapioca), palm oil, sugarcane, bananas; sheep, goats; timber

Industry (5.4% of GDP): rubber processing, palm oil processing, timber, diamonds

Services (17.7% of GDP): government, other

Foreign trade:
   Exports–$910 million: rubber, timber, iron, diamonds, cocoa, coffee (2004 est.)
   Imports–$4.839 billion: fuels, chemicals, machinery, transportation equipment, manufactured goods; foodstuffs (2004 est.)

Economic growth rate: 6.7%

Currency exchange rate: U.S. $1 = 49 Liberian dollars (2007)

*GDP is the total value of goods and services produced in a country annually.
All figures are 2006 estimates unless otherwise indicated.
Source: CIA World Factbook, 2007.

in 2002 was $561.8 million—a figure that represented just 45.9 percent of the GDP before fighting broke out in 1989. Although the GDP climbed back to $2.9 billion in 2006, much of this wealth is concentrated in the hands of a few people. The majority of Liberians live on an average of 25 cents a day.

Affording a simple life is an enormous challenge in Liberia. The population faces an 80 to 85 percent unemployment rate, and the United Nations estimates that over 80 percent of Liberians live below the poverty line. People also struggle to afford basic commodities. A bag of rice is sold at $22 to $30, while the average worker only earns between $10 and $20 per month.

The country's health and education services are no better. In October 2005 journalist Joe S. Kappia reported that 30 Liberian medical doctors were serving over 3 million people, and a UN panel found that an understaffed teaching force had gone 24 months without receiving pay.

Making a Living

Most of Liberia's wealth comes from its soil, as roughly 70 percent of the labor force is made up of farmers or plantation workers. A large portion of Liberia's land is ideal for tree crops such as coffee, cacao, palm oil, coconuts, and rubber. Of these, rubber is the biggest cash crop, and rubber plantations are the largest private-sector employer in the country.

Liberian rubber is produced by large corporations as well as *smallholders*, who generate about 30 percent of the total rubber output. The industry first took off in 1926, the year the Firestone Tire and Rubber Company signed a lease for a million acres of land just east of Monrovia. The benefits were enormous for the company, which obtained the 90-year lease for six cents per acre. It used some of its profits to build up infrastructure, constructing hospitals and a road network that connected Liberia with Guinea and the Ivory Coast. The Firestone plantation soon became the largest industrial rubber plantation in the world, and it maintains that distinction today.

Although the rubber industry thrived for decades, it faced serious production setbacks during the civil war. The International Monetary Fund (IMF) estimated that earnings generated from Liberian rubber fell from $73.5 million in 1988 to as low as $2.4 million during the first half of the war. After a brief recovery, rubber earnings fell again from $59.2 million in 2002 to $38.4 million in 2003.

The decline in production was the result of rebel looting and a lack of sustainable practices. During the war plantations underwent barely any replanting, which is an essential practice in rubber production because older trees yield significantly lower levels of latex. But in 2005 Firestone, which now operates under the Japanese-owned Bridgestone, came up with a redevelopment strategy. After renewing the land lease for another 36 years, the company reported its plan to give smallholders 600,000 rubber stumps to help them replant their plantations. General manager Charles Stuart also announced that Firestone will invest more than $100 million in the industry.

Another major industry is iron ore mining, which primarily takes place in the Nimba Range; in the Bomi Hills and Bong Range in the central region; and at Cape Mount on the Mano River. At one point iron ore pulled in more revenue annually than rubber and provided 47 percent of the country's export earnings. However, during the war some mines were damaged and production was halted, while others were seized by the NPFL and other factions. Many foreign investors still have not returned, and a number of iron mining operations remain closed today.

Diamonds are Liberia's other major mineral export. But diamond revenue has been frozen as a result of a UN embargo that has been extended several times since it was first imposed in 2001. The diamonds are traditionally mined in the Lofa and Nimba counties in the northern half of the country. According to an August 2001 story published in the *New York Times*, in 2000,

The Bong iron mine, pictured here, is located north of Monrovia. Although iron ore remains in the ground, the mine was shut down during the civil war and has never reopened.

while the NPFL still traded arms for diamonds with the RUF, Liberia unlawfully exported an estimated $300 million in diamonds, only some of which originated in Liberian soil (most were mined in Sierra Leone). Today, if diamond firms could meet the costs of trade certification and convince the UN to lift the embargo, Liberian diamond exports could bring in $10 million or more annually.

Timber is another valuable resource, although its earning potential has been wasted through government corruption and mismanagement. In response to illegal logging practices, the United Nations imposed a separate embargo on timber in 2003. This sanction could have been imposed earlier but was delayed due to pressure from France and China, two major customers for Liberian timber.

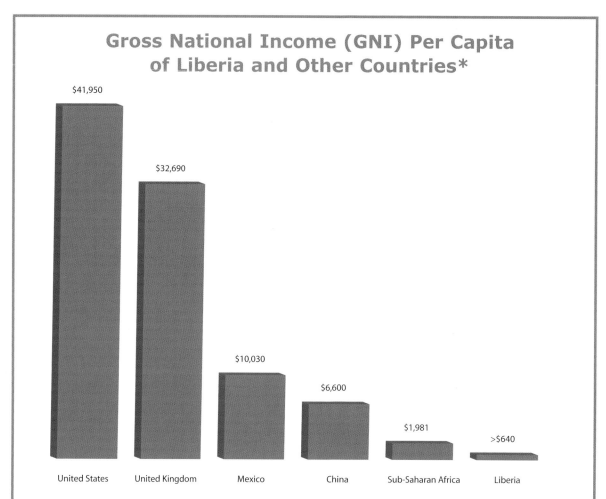

Gross National Income (GNI) Per Capita of Liberia and Other Countries*

- United States — $41,950
- United Kingdom — $32,690
- Mexico — $10,030
- China — $6,600
- Sub-Saharan Africa — $1,981
- Liberia — >$640

*Gross national income per capita is the total value of all goods and services produced domestically in a year, supplemented by income received from abroad, divided by midyear population. The above figures take into account fluctuations in currency exchange rates and differences in inflation rates across global economies.

All figures are based on 2005 data. Source: World Bank, 2006.

Experts have reported that the illegal timber trade fueled the civil war just as much, if not more, than diamonds. Patrick Alley, director of the human rights and environmental group Global Witness, estimated that the timber trade under Taylor brought in as much as $187 million a year, although the government only declared a fraction of this amount. During its two-year existence, the National Transition Government of Liberia failed to complete all the reforms needed to lift the embargo, which was extended once again in December 2005.

Industry Mainstays

One source of revenue that remained steady even during the fighting is the national merchant marine. For several decades, Liberia's large shipping fleet, which is only outnumbered by the fleets of Panama and China, has been a reliable revenue source. In 2004 Liberia earned more than $15 million from its fleet of more than 1,800 vessels.

Most of these ships are not actually Liberian but sail under its national flag. This arrangement was set up through the adoption of the 1948 Maritime Code, which permits foreign ships from Germany, Greece, the United States, and other countries to register as Liberian vessels. In exchange for paying the registry fee, shipping companies can avoid the wage requirements on the seamen they hire from Liberia and other developing countries. Human rights groups have complained that this employment system does not ensure good working conditions on the boats.

Another major revenue source during and since the war has been *remittances*. Individuals living and working in the United States and other countries send home on average about $2 million a month.

Essential Changes

Regardless of whether foreign assistance comes from family members or other governments, it is pivotal to the reconstruction of Liberia's battered infrastructure and the improvement of basic services like education and health care. Much-needed funds were generated in 2004 when a major donor conference in New York pledged over $500 million for renovations.

Foreign investment is also needed to redevelop the main export industries. This will not be easy since many companies closed up and pulled out

Liberia is rebuilding its economy with international assistance. At this 2004 meeting, the United Nations and the World Bank promised more than $500 million for urgent reconstruction needs.

of the country during the war. Were the government to clamp down on the ongoing illegal trade of timber and diamonds, causing the UN to lift its sanctions, it is more likely that foreign companies would establish operations once again.

Equally crucial to Liberia's welfare are reforms that would ultimately make the economic system less dependent on foreign dollars. Currently, the country is disadvantaged by its lack of local manufacturing. Many Liberians lack the skills and technical means for the manufacturing sector to develop. The implementation of a more skilled workforce would increase domestic production and make the Liberian economy more resilient against trade embargos and fluctuations in the world market.

Visitors to Liberia can observe great diversity among the country's many ethnic groups. (Opposite) Young students assemble to salute the flag outside a Catholic school. (Right) Liberians wearing traditional garb perform on a street in Monrovia.

5 Bridging the Divide

THROUGHOUT MUCH OF LIBERIA'S HISTORY, the majority of Americo-Liberians preserved the great divide between themselves and the country's indigenous peoples. Their wealth, sophistication, and Christian faith distinguished them from the tribespeople of the interior. Americo-Liberians generally are wealthier than native Liberians, and they tend to live in the coastal towns and outlying regions. However, for some years the cultural gap has been gradually closing between these two groups, and as a result, they are moving closer toward forming a shared Liberian culture.

Making up only 2.5 percent of the population, the Liberian descendants of the freed slaves have exercised a great amount of influence in spite of their small numbers. Today this group shuns the label "Americo-Liberian," which to some suggests they do not have firm roots in their own country.

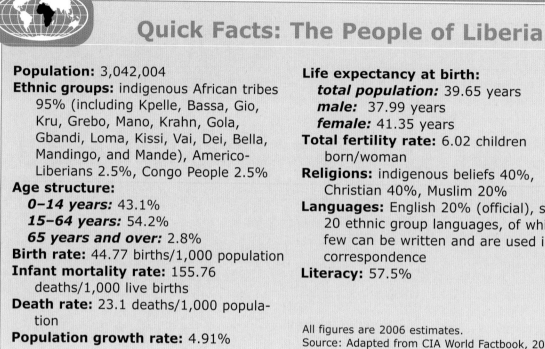

Quick Facts: The People of Liberia

Population: 3,042,004

Ethnic groups: indigenous African tribes 95% (including Kpelle, Bassa, Gio, Kru, Grebo, Mano, Krahn, Gola, Gbandi, Loma, Kissi, Vai, Dei, Bella, Mandingo, and Mande), Americo-Liberians 2.5%, Congo People 2.5%

Age structure:
  0–14 years: 43.1%
  15–64 years: 54.2%
  65 years and over: 2.8%

Birth rate: 44.77 births/1,000 population

Infant mortality rate: 155.76 deaths/1,000 live births

Death rate: 23.1 deaths/1,000 population

Population growth rate: 4.91%

Life expectancy at birth:
  total population: 39.65 years
  male: 37.99 years
  female: 41.35 years

Total fertility rate: 6.02 children born/woman

Religions: indigenous beliefs 40%, Christian 40%, Muslim 20%

Languages: English 20% (official), some 20 ethnic group languages, of which a few can be written and are used in correspondence

Literacy: 57.5%

All figures are 2006 estimates.
Source: Adapted from CIA World Factbook, 2007.

A separate group descended from a people known as the Congos makes up another 2.5 percent of the population. The Congos, or "recaptives," were slaves from the Congo region of Central Africa, parts of West Africa, and the Angola region who had regained their freedom before reaching the New World. They were not, however, sent back to their places of origin, but rather redirected to Liberia and the surrounding area. Because Americo-Liberians claimed similar origins with the Congos, over time they more readily assimilated the recaptives into their culture.

The rest of the population is made up of at least 16 ethnic groups who speak more than 20 languages and local dialects. Some *ethnologists* say there are as many as 14 more groups besides those officially recognized.

Identifying these groups is difficult because many of the government-created labels for tribes were applied more out of a need to establish territorial lines than to accurately identify people. Outsiders refer to one group as the Krahn, for example, though these people rarely use this label to refer to themselves.

Another reason why identifying distinct groups is difficult is that a number of tribes have been assimilated into others. This process has been shaped by forces like urbanization, intermingling, and population shifts due to new job opportunities. One distinguishing cultural feature that commonly has been altered is language, and in some cases, languages have been replaced altogether.

The Major Ethnic Groups

The Kpelle are Liberia's largest ethnic group, numbering over 300,000 people. They reside in central and western Liberia, mainly in Bong County, as well as in urban communities like Monrovia, where there are distinct Kpelle communities. They are believed to have migrated in the 16th century from the region of modern-day Guinea and today live under 12 chiefdoms.

The Kru, historically a seafaring people, generally live on Liberia's coast and the interior regions of Sinoe County, which is home of the Greenville port. During the Age of Exploration, Europeans hired Kru as seamen on trading vessels and warships. Historians surmise that the Kru are among the oldest

A Kru family looks out from a window of their home on the coast.

established ethnic groups and thus have incorporated other groups into their communities over the centuries.

A geographically scattered group, the Krahn have formed six chiefdoms in Sinoe, Nimba, and Grand Gedeh County. There are also Krahn members living in the Ivory Coast, where they are referred to as the Wee. The NPFL, which considered the Krahn to be loyal supporters of President Doe, focused its attacks on Krahn villages in the beginning of its 1989 campaign. During the second half of the civil war, many Krahn joined the MODEL army and supported its crusade to overthrow the Taylor government.

The Mandingo, who settled in the western region in the 17th century, were among the first to connect the interior with the Atlantic trade. They came in larger waves in the late 19th and early 20th centuries after the Wassoulou Empire in Guinea fell to colonial forces. They were once led by the great Muslim ruler Almamy Samory Touré, whose empire covered parts of what became Sierra Leone, Guinea, and Ivory Coast. Today many Mandingo remain in western Liberia, situated in two chiefdoms in Bomi and Lofa Counties, while other enclaves are found in Gbarnga, Monrovia, and other urban centers. The Mandingo have remained a group set apart because of their Islamic faith and their reputation as traders. With the Mende, Gola, Gbandi, and a large segment of the Lebanese minority, the Mandingo form the 20 percent of the population that makes up the Muslim minority.

The Three Religions

While the Mandingo's traditions are strongly grounded in Islam, Liberian groups like the Mende, Gola, and Gbandi have preserved their own indigenous traditions as they have gradually adopted Islamic beliefs. Similarly, other groups have assimilated Christian elements into their original belief systems. A relatively small segment of Liberians—roughly 20 percent—practice only indigenous religions in their pure forms.

Liberia's Muslims, who are nearly all followers of the orthodox Sunni branch, live mostly in the western and central regions, with some pockets settled in the eastern region. There are more than a half dozen mosques in Monrovia, and 100 more scattered throughout the rest of the country. Unlike in other African societies where Muslims have clashed with Christians, Liberian Muslims have enjoyed a relatively peaceful *coexistence* with citizens of other faiths.

The Christian faith has figured prominently in the lives of the settlers and their descendants, as well as those segments of the present-day indigenous population that have come in contact with church representatives and converts. The Christian mindset is strongly reflected in the country's main governing documents, including the 1986 constitution, which asserts Liberia's "reliance on 'His Divine Guidance' for its survival."

The Christian segment of the Liberian population is very diverse, made up of grassroots churches as well as traditional parishes of the Catholic and mainstream Protestant denominations. Many indigenous Liberians distinguish churches as *kwi*, a label referring to a formal style of worship. In recent years more *Pentecostal* and *Charismatic* churches, which are not *kwi*, have sprung up. Their worship style is marked by acts of physical healing and a "direct experience of the Holy Spirit."

The dramatic worship style embraced by Pentecostal and Charismatic Christians resembles the practices of indigenous traditions—a fact that has helped indigenous peoples assimilate the Western faith into their beliefs. In some communities it is not uncommon for a leader to take on the dual role of Christian deacon and *zo*, the Liberian term for village priest.

However, in many areas indigenous traditions have undergone minimal change, particularly the secret societies prevalent among the ethnic groups in Liberia and other West African nations. The secret nature of these societies derives not from their membership, which is generally open, but rather the

A Liberian Christian prays during a Pentecostal church service. About 40 percent of Liberians are Christians, although many Liberian Christians also observe traditional African religious rites.

undisclosed rituals of the groups' rites of passage, as well as the secret powers and training that their zoes possess.

Most of these societies are organized by gender: male societies are known as Poro and female are Sande. (Other societies may go by different names but are similarly grouped by gender.) Poro and Sande traditions deal mainly with the spirits of ancestors, animals, or natural surroundings.

During a special initiation that takes place at puberty, boys go through a set of rituals and a period of rebirth in which they commune with the spirits of the forest. Sometime during these sessions of "bush school," which are held in a restricted area of the forest, the old selves of the boys are said to be eaten by the Bush Devil (though fearsome, this forest spirit is not as evil as its name implies). Villagers celebrate the boys' graduation from bush school and their passage into manhood by smearing their faces with white clay, a symbol of their rebirth.

The principal task of the *zo* is to represent spirits to the tribe, which occurs through the mask ritual. The mask, which is usually carved from wood, is a religious relic with special powers. By wearing the mask and camouflaging himself completely to hide his normal appearance, the *zo* makes himself ready to be briefly possessed by a spirit, which may then reveal a prophecy about a community's future.

The Arts

Traditional Liberian dance, unlike Western styles, is not readily distinguished from religious ritual; thus, music and dancing commonly accompany the Poro mask ritual. Dancing in Liberia is marked by a high level of athleticism and exuberance, and every tribe has its own signature dance steps. Performances are typically accompanied by log drums, whose earthy sound is reminiscent of the sounds of the forest and its spirits.

Liberia's musical heritage contains diverse elements, including Latin American *genres*, the choral singing of Western missionaries, and West African music, which is characterized by the combination of multiple

Poro masks like these are used in some traditional religious rites. The masks are believed to channel the power of ancestors, linking the wearer with the spirit world and the Supreme Being.

rhythms, ululation (high-pitched warbling), and call-and-response between singer and chorus. The origins of Highlife music, a West African genre that incorporates Cuban rumba and other forms of Latin music, is attributed to the Kru. Traveling along the West African coast centuries ago, Kru sailors played music with some of the small portable instruments that are synonymous with Highlife today, including the accordion, harmonica, mandolin, and the Spanish guitar.

In addition to dance, Liberia also has a tradition of creative writing. The most prominent of Liberia's writers have also been leaders. Roland Dempster (1910–65), a poet, was a representative from Grand Cape Mount County. The folklorist Bai T. Moore (1920–88) served as the chief of the Bureau of Agriculture. More recently, playwright and author Wilton Sankawulo (born 1937) chaired the Council of State of the transitional government that was in place between 1995 and 1996. One of Sankawulo's most well-known works is *The Marriage of Wisdom*, an anthology of Liberian folk tales published in 1974.

Education

Many of Liberia's leaders consider educational reform critical to the country's postwar reconstruction. Faced with a literacy rate estimated somewhere between 60 and 85 percent, reformers have a long road ahead of them. One of the most urgent projects has been rebuilding the University of Liberia in Monrovia, which suffered major looting during the civil war. Dating back to 1863, the university is one of West Africa's oldest institutes of higher learning. The school reopened in 2005 with hopes of building capacity for more

Liberian students, many of whom would otherwise receive their education in the United States.

Another school with a great educational legacy is Cuttington University College at Suakoko, a town 120 miles (193 km) north of Monrovia. Founded by the Episcopal Church, it is the oldest private, coeducational, four-year, degree-granting university in sub-Saharan Africa.

More than 40 percent of Liberia's population lives in the capital city, Monrovia. (Opposite) An aerial view of the city's skyline, with the Atlantic Ocean visible in the background. (Right) A bridal party is photographed in front of a monument to former president Joseph Jenkins Roberts.

6 Cities and Communities

A LARGE NUMBER of the nearly 3.5 million Liberians living in the country are settled on the coast, where all the major towns except Gbarnga are located. Liberia's major port towns are Buchanan, Greenville, Harper, and the capital city, Monrovia, which dwarfs the others in population and size. During the war years, urban populations swelled as thousands of uprooted people arrived to escape the fighting.

Monrovia

Liberia's capital and main commercial center lies on one of the country's few peninsulas, in the northwest region at the mouths of the Mesurado and St. Paul rivers. The city is home to an estimated 600,000 residents. Because the city was originally built to accommodate only 400,000 people, many households have been forced to go without running water or electricity.

Long before the American Colonization Society arrived at Cape Mesurado in 1821, the Dei and Bassa were settled there. After bullying the tribes into offering up their land, the colonists settled on tiny Providence Island, located near what is now downtown Monrovia. From there they moved onto the mainland and named the new community after James

A view of the city center of Monrovia. Many people living in the city do not have access to running water or electricity in their homes.

Monroe, the fifth president of the United States and an ACS supporter. A couple of decades later, Monrovia became the capital of the new republic of Liberia.

Monrovia received an economic boost from the U.S.-led construction of the city's deepwater port, which took place between 1944 and 1948. A port industry has since developed at the Freeport at Bushrod Island, located just north of the capital. There, exporters send out iron ore and use the Freeport's warehouses to store petroleum and liquid rubber latex. Trading outfits from prosperous nations also use the port as a place to dock their ships for repair and to transfer goods headed for other destinations along the West African coast. Liberians have flocked from the interior to the capital in search of the jobs this industry has created.

Other people have found jobs at the Firestone plantation and its *company town*, Harbel, located 32 miles (51 km) southeast of Monrovia. Named after company founder Harvey Firestone and his wife Idabelle, Harbel is home to most of the plantation's workers. Firestone manages the town's hospital and hydroelectric power plant as well as its roads, housing, and school system.

This new economy that the Freeport and the rubber plantation spawned was seriously derailed by the fighting between 1989 and 2003. A major battle took place in Monrovia in 1990, when the INPFL, a splinter group of NPFL, attacked President's Doe stronghold. In 1992 the NPFL launched an offensive on the city. In 2003, during the campaign to bring down President Taylor, the LURD rebel army briefly had control of the Freeport before relinquishing it as part of the August peace agreement.

Now that peace is restored, Monrovians are eager to finish the city's reconstruction. Much of the rebuilding is focused on downtown Monrovia, located south of Freeport along the banks of the Mesurado River. This district features the University of Liberia, the Executive Mansion, and the National Museum. Originally the home of President Joseph Jenkins Roberts, the National Museum served as the house of the national legislature from the 19th century through the 20th century. Today the museum promotes indigenous culture with a collection of historic and cultural artifacts.

Another important cultural archive, the National Cultural Center, is found in Kendeja, located just 10 miles (16 km) down the shore from Monrovia. The center exhibits the architecture of the country's major ethnic groups.

Gbarnga

Gbarnga (estimated population: 45,835) is Liberia's second most populous city and the capital of Bong County, which sits between the counties of the coast and the Guinean border. A main road from Monrovia runs through this small city, connecting the region with the Ivory Coast and Guinea.

Gbarnga serves as an administrative center and trade hub for the interior. Local industries include commercial poultry farming and a rubber factory, which since 1976 has processed latex into crumb rubber, a material used in asphalt and various rubber products.

The city contains a large Mandingo enclave, while the surrounding region is the homeland of the Kpelle people. Living in these close quarters, the two groups have clashed at different points in history. Gbarnga suffered the worst of the calamities during the periods when various rebel forces sought its capture in the quest to establish control over the interior. It served as a temporary capital of Liberia when the INPFL controlled a large portion of the country and was briefly taken again by LURD forces in March 2003. On several occasions during the fighting, Cuttington University, located 10 miles (16 km) west of Gbarnga, had to close its doors and hold classes at another location until peace was restored.

Buchanan

The second-largest port in Liberia is Buchanan, which has a population of about 25,700. The capital of Grand Bassa County, this town lies 62 miles (100 km) southeast of Monrovia, near the mouth of the St. John River.

In the 19th century, long before the city had a deepwater port, Buchanan was an export site for palm oil and piassava fiber, a tough kind of fiber used to make mats and ropes. In later decades mining companies identified the port as a place to export the iron ore that was being mined in the mineral-rich Nimba Range in the northern region. During the 1960s the Liberian American-Swedish Minerals Company (LAMCO) built the port facility and laid down a 168-mile (270-km) railroad connecting the port to the mines. The rail line suffered neglect for years, however, and still has not been rebuilt.

Harper

The county seat of Maryland County, Harper (estimated population: 32,661) is situated on Cape Palmas near the Ivory Coast. Before the UN ban on timber was imposed on Liberia, Harper coordinated with the Greenville port,

A young child stands in front of his dilapidated home in Buchanan. The city is the second-largest port in Liberia.

which lies 124 miles (200 km) west, to export much of the timber produced in the surrounding region.

The Harper settlement was established as a separate mission of the Maryland State Colonization Society (MSCS). The town was the capital of the independent State of Maryland in Africa before it became a county seat of the new Liberian republic in 1854. A century later, Harper was folded into the developing national economy with the construction of its harbor and the opening of the road to Monrovia.

Harper enjoyed periods of relative peace during the war years. Because of this, it has welcomed thousands of refugees, many of them individuals fleeing the domestic conflict that raged in the Ivory Coast between 2002 and 2005. Two months before MODEL forces captured Harper in May 2003, the Harper region was hosting about 38,000 Ivorian refugees and about 45,000 Liberians returning to their homes.

A Calendar of Liberian Festivals

January

Pioneers' Day, observed on January 7, remembers the white settlers and freed black settlers who in the 19th century arrived to the land that became Liberia. It is a controversial holiday that some Liberians do not celebrate.

February

On February 11, **Armed Forces Day**, Liberians honor the nation's army, navy, and militia.

March

Decoration Day on March 13 is an occasion to display the national flag, known as the "Lone Star." On March 15 Liberians celebrate the birthday of Joseph Jenkins Roberts, the republic's first president.

April

Fast and Prayer Day, which takes place on the second Friday of April, is a day for religious devotion.

Liberians honor April 12 as **National Redemption Day**, the anniversary of the 1980 coup led by Samuel Doe. Although Doe's presidency was marked by abuse and scandal, Liberians recognize the coup as a turning point for the long-repressed indigenous majority.

July

Liberians at home and abroad celebrate **Independence Day** on July 26 with beauty pageants and sports competitions. In the United States immigrants have begun a tradition of hosting an annual soccer tournament between rival Liberian teams the Invincible Eleven and the Mighty Barrolle.

August

Flag Day, held on August 24, is another occasion to show Liberian patriotism. People hang the Liberian flag in public buildings and participate in parades.

November

Liberians show their gratitude for the things they have on **Thanksgiving Day**, observed on the first Thursday of November.

William V. S. Tubman's Birthday, November 9, is a holiday that the leader himself started during his 27-year presidency. Many Liberians spend this day, also known as **Goodwill Day**, at the beach.

December

On December 1, **Matilda Newport Day**, some citizens remember the famous Americo-

Liberian woman who some believe fought in a successful campaign against the natives. According to the myth, she fired a cannon at enemy lines by lighting it with her pipe.

Liberian Christians celebrate **Christmas** on December 25.

Religious Holidays

Liberia's Christians and Muslims observe some important holy days that fall on different dates each year. This is because they are determined by the phases of the moon, rather than based on the 365-day solar calendar.

For Roman Catholics, the holiest season of the year is known as **Lent**. This is a 40-day period leading up to **Easter** during which Christians are expected to think about Jesus Christ's sacrifice on the cross. The last week of Lent is known as Passion Week, and recognizes the arrival of Jesus in Jerusalem on **Palm Sunday**, the Last Supper on **Holy Thursday**, and the crucifixion on **Good Friday**. These are followed by **Easter Sunday**, when Christians celebrate the resurrection of Jesus. The dates of these holidays vary from year to year, depending on the full moon; Easter always falls between March 22 and April 25. The Monday after Easter is also a public holiday.

For Liberian Muslims, the dates of their holy days are determined by the Islamic lunar calendar. There are 354 days in each lunar year, which is divided into 12 months. Since the lunar year is 11 days shorter than the solar year, religious holidays occur on different days every year.

Islamic New Year is celebrated on the first day of Muharram, the first month of the lunar calendar.

Ramadan, an important holiday observed during the ninth lunar month, is a time of sacrifice for Muslims. Between sunrise and sunset they abstain from eating and drinking; Liberian Muslims also stop listening to music. A *papali* performs the special duty of walking from door to door to wake up families for a late meal called the *suhoor*. Before eating the meal they will recite a prayer known as the Shahadah.

At the end of Ramadan, Muslims celebrate **Eid al-Fitr**, or the Feast of Fast-Breaking. During this day families get together and exchange gifts.

Eid al-Adha is a holiday commemorating the patriarch Abraham's willingness to sacrifice his son to God. On this day, which takes place during the final month of the Muslim calendar, Liberians who can afford to will sacrifice a sheep or a cow to remember Abraham's act of loyalty. Muslims also attend their local mosques, where religious leaders known as imams lead prayers to Allah.

Recipes

Jollof Rice

cooked meats (such as chicken, bacon, shrimp, or smoked pork)
1/2 cup yellow onions
1/2 cup green peppers
1/2 tsp. ground ginger
1/4 cup vegetable oil
One 16 oz. can whole tomatoes
Two 6 oz. cans tomato paste
2 quarts water
salt and pepper
1/2 tsp. thyme
1 tsp. crushed red pepper
5 cups chicken stock or water

Directions:

1. Cut the meats into 1-inch chunks and sauté in vegetable oil until slightly brown. In a 4-quart pot, sauté ginger, onions, and peppers in oil. Add tomatoes and simmer for 5 minutes.
2. Add tomato paste, water, and seasonings. Add the cooked meat and simmer 20 minutes longer. Correct the seasonings with salt, pepper, and other ingredients.
3. In a 2-quart saucepan, cook rice in chicken stock or water until tender. Pour rice in a deep bowl, then pour sauce of the meat over it, arranging the meat in the center.

Monrovian Collards and Cabbage (serves 8)

1 bunch collard greens, washed and cut in small pieces
2 lbs. cabbage, cut into 8 wedges
1/2 lb. bacon, cut into 1- to 2-inch pieces
1 large onion, sliced
1 tbs. salt
1 tbs. crushed red pepper
1 tsp. black pepper
1 oz. butter or oil
1 quart water

Directions:

1. In a 4-quart saucepan, combine collard greens, onion, salt, red pepper, black pepper, and water and simmer gently for 30 minutes.
2. Add cabbage and butter or oil. Cook for 15 minutes or until vegetables are tender. Season to taste. Strain before serving if water has not been absorbed.
3. Serve in a 2-quart bowl.

Liberian Sweet Potato Pone

3 cups grated raw sweet potatoes
1 cup molasses or dark cane syrup
2 tsp. ground ginger
2 tsp. baking powder
1 tsp. salt
1/3 cup vegetable oil

Directions:

1. In a 3-quart saucepan, combine all ingredients and simmer slowly, stirring constantly, for 10 minutes. Pour into well-greased 9-inch baking pan.
2. Bake at 325°F for 30 minutes, stirring every 5 minutes for the first 20 minutes. Smooth down the top and allow to brown.
3. Cut into squares and serve either hot or cold.

Ginger Beer (makes more than 2.5 gallons)

1 lb. fresh ginger, finely chopped and then beat to a powder
2 fresh pineapples, unpeeled and cut in chunks
2 gallons boiling water
2 tsp. yeast
3 1/2 cups molasses

Directions:

1. Combine pineapples and ginger. Pour water over the ingredients and allow to cool to luke-warm.
2. Add yeast dissolved in 1/2 cup of water. Allow to stand overnight covered. Add molasses on the following day. Ginger beer may be diluted with water or extra sugar, or ginger may be added to obtain desired taste.

Stewed Mangoes with Cloves

4 large mangos
1 cup syrup from a can of peaches
6 whole cloves

Directions:

1. Peel mangos and cut in large pieces. Place in sauté pan. Add syrup and cloves.
2. Simmer for 15 minutes or until mangos are tender. Spear some of the pieces with a few cloves.
3. Cool and serve.

Glossary

abolitionists—individuals who advocate the end of slavery.

bicameral—consisting of two legislative chambers.

Charismatic—Christians who believe that the manifestations of the Holy Spirit seen in early Christianity, such as healings and speaking in tongues, can be witnessed today.

coexistence—the state of living in peace with each other.

company town—a community that is dependent on one company for all or most of its services or functions.

despot—a ruler who governs with absolute power and authority.

dispossession—the act of taking someone's possessions or claims to land.

ecologist—a person who studies the relationship between living organisms and their environment.

embargo—legal prohibition on commerce.

ethnologists—scientists who deal with the division of human beings into races.

genre—a category of art, music, or writing characterized by a particular style, form, or content.

gross domestic product (GDP)—the total value of goods and services produced in a country in a one-year period.

hierarchy—a body of persons having authority.

hydroelectric—relating to the production of electricity by waterpower.

indigenous—having originated and lived in a particular region.

infractions—violations.

infrastructure—the system of public works of a country, state, or region.

judiciary—a system of courts of law.

maritime—of or relating to navigation or commerce on the sea.

one-party state—a country in which a single ruling party makes all decisions and its authority goes unchallenged.

Pentecostal—similar to Charismatic churches, Pentecostals believe in the miracles of the Holy Spirit and specifically believe that those baptized in the Holy Spirit will speak in tongues.

promontory—a high point of land or rock projecting into a body of water.

provisional—under terms not final or fully worked out or agreed upon; temporary.

remittances—a sum of money sent back to friends or family in a person's homeland.

sanctions—economic measures collectively adopted by several nations to force a particular nation to stop practices deemed in violation of international law.

smallholders—people owning or renting small farms.

sovereignty—freedom from external control.

Project and Report Ideas

Reports

The Special Court of Sierra Leone has indicted former president Charles Taylor and other Liberians of war crimes and crimes against humanity. Another court in Africa, the International Criminal Tribunal for Rwanda (ICTR), has prosecuted individuals for similar crimes. In a one-page report, explain why courts like these have been set up and what they have accomplished thus far. Be sure to identify the crimes that are being prosecuted.

Other West African countries besides Liberia have experienced civil wars in recent decades. Research one of these conflicts and write a report that explains how the civil war broke out. Give background on all the major players involved, and devote a paragraph or two of your report to explaining how the fighting in your selected country affected Liberia or how Liberia became involved in the war.

Maps

Make a map showing all 15 of Liberia's rivers. Include the names of the ports that are located near or at the mouths of the major rivers.

Draw a map showing the regions where the following resources are found in Liberia: iron ore, diamonds, timber, rubber.

Biographies

Write a one-page report about one of the following figures in Liberian history:

Joseph Jenkins Roberts

William V. S. Tubman

William R. Tolbert, Jr.

Samuel Doe

Amos Sawyer

Charles Taylor

George Weah

Ellen Johnson-Sirleaf

Project and Report Ideas

Endangered Species Presentation

Liberia's rain forest, which is part of the Upper Guinea Forest, is home to several rare species of plants and animals whose existence is being threatened by excessive logging. Draw or cut out pictures of two of these species and write a short description that includes their defining characteristics. Present your poster to your classmates and explain what ecologists and others are doing to save the wildlife from extinction.

Experience the Culture

Internet sites are available to those who want to learn more about the Highlife music of Liberia. Read up on this music genre and find audio samples to play for classmates. Be prepared to identify at least two musical elements of Highlife and their countries or regions of origin.

Creative Project

Civil war has kept Liberia from expanding its tourism industry, but a new peace holds promise for this sector. Research Internet sites devoted to travel in Liberia and then write a three-paragraph pitch highlighting the country's main attractions.

Chronology

1300s–1400s:	Mel-speaking peoples from the north arrive in the land that became Liberia.
1455:	Mande-speaking peoples, who were traders from the same empires as the Mel-speakers, begin migrating to the region.
1461:	The first Portuguese explorers land on the Liberian coast.
1500s–1800s:	Portuguese and other European explorers engage with tribes of the interior to trade for cloth, ivory, gold, palm oil, and slaves.
1820–21:	Supported by the American Colonization Society, settlers arrive at Cape Palmas. After two failed attempts, the colony of Liberia is established.
1831:	The Maryland State Colonization Society founds a colony near Cape Palmas.
1839:	The colony of Liberia becomes the Commonwealth of Liberia.
1847:	After declaring its independence, Liberia becomes a free republic and ratifies a new constitution.
1855:	Ethnic Kru clash with settlers in a conflict known as the Sinoe War.
1875–76:	The Grebo people fight for and win full Liberian citizenship.
1892:	France gives Liberia 25,000 francs as part of agreement settling the country's eastern border.
1904:	President Arthur Barclay introduces a plan to divide national districts along ethnic lines.
1943:	The United States and Liberia sign the Mutual Aid Agreement, paving the way for the construction of the country's first artificial deepwater port in Monrovia.
1944:	William V. S. Tubman is elected and introduces his Open Door Policy to encourage foreign investment.
1971:	After reigning for 27 years, President Tubman dies and is succeeded by William R. Tolbert.
1979:	Violent demonstrations known as the Rice Riots erupt in response to Tolbert's proposal to raise the price of imported rice.

Chronology

1980: Samuel Doe leads a coup to overthrow President Tolbert; in addition to killing Tolbert, his People's Redemption Council murders 26 government leaders and later publicly executes 13 cabinet members.

1986: The National Constitutional Commission, established by President Doe, ratifies a new constitution that finally includes Liberia's indigenous population in the voting process.

1989: On Christmas Eve, Charles Taylor leads his rebel army, the National Patriotic Front of Liberia (NPFL), in an invasion of Liberia to overthrow President Doe.

1993: The Cotonou Peace Agreement establishes a transitional government and sets up the United Nations Observer Mission in Liberia (UNMIL).

1996: In April, factions clash in a battle in Monrovia that claims 5,000 people; a peace accord signed in Abuja, Nigeria, implements a disarmament plan and sets a timetable for a presidential election the following year.

1997: Charles Taylor is elected president in August.

1999: Liberians United for Reconciliation and Democracy (LURD), a group pursuing the overthrow of President Taylor, forms in Guinea and launches a rebellion.

2000: The United Nations issues embargoes on the export of diamonds and guns from Liberia.

2003: The United Nations issues ban on the export of Liberian timber; Taylor, increasingly threatened by advancing rebel groups, finally agrees to resign and escapes to exile in August; during the same month rebel groups sign peace accord and agree to the creation of a transitional government.

2005: In November, Ellen Johnson-Sirleaf wins run-off election against George Weah; in December, the United Nations renews its diamond and timber embargos on Liberia.

2006: In January, Johnson-Sirleaf becomes the first woman president in Africa.

2007: UNMIL continues with its peacemaking operations.

Further Reading/Internet Resources

Ellis, Stephen. *The Mask of Anarchy: The Destruction of Liberia and the Religious Dimension of an African Civil War.* London: Hurst & Company, 1999.

Nelson, Harold D, ed. *Liberia: A Country Study.* Washington, D.C.: Foreign Area Studies, American University, 1984.

Pham, John-Peter. *Liberia: Portrait of a Failed State.* New York: Reed Press, 2004.

Reef, Catherine. *This Our Dark Country: The American Settlers of Liberia.* New York: Clarion Books, 2002.

Yoder, John C. *Popular Political Culture, Civil Society, and State Crisis in Liberia.* Lewiston, New York: Edwin Mellen Press, 2003.

Travel Information

http://www.lonelyplanet.com/worldguide/destinations/africa/liberia
http://www.traveldocs.com/lr/index.htm

History and Geography

http://www.pbs.org/wgbh/globalconnections/liberia/
http://www.infoplease.com/ipa/A0107718.html

Economic and Political Information

http://www.state.gov/r/pa/ei/bgn/6618.htm
http://www.globalsecurity.org/military/library/report/1985/liberia_contents.htm

Culture and Festivals

http://www.liberianforum.com/index.htm
http://www.culturalpartnerships.org/ontour/liberia.asp

U.S. Embassy in Liberia
111 UN Drive
PO Box 98
Monrovia, Liberia
Tel: (+231) 77-054-826
E-mail: ConsularMonrovia@state.gov
Website: http://usembassy.state.gov/liberia/

Liberian Ministry of Information, Culture, and Tourism
PO Box 10-9021
Monrovia, Liberia
Tel: (+231) 226-269
Fax: (+231) 226-045
Website: http://www.micat.gov.lr

Embassy of the Republic of Liberia
5201 16th Street, NW
Washington, D.C. 20011
Tel: (202) 723-0437
Fax: (202) 723-0436
E-mail: info@embassyofliberia.org
Website: http://www.embassyofliberia.org

Index

Numbers in **bold italic** refer to captions.

Contributors/Picture Credits

Professor Robert I. Rotberg is Director of the Program on Intrastate Conflict and Conflict Resolution at the Kennedy School, Harvard University, and President of the World Peace Foundation. He is the author of a number of books and articles on Africa, including *A Political History of Tropical Africa* and *Ending Autocracy, Enabling Democracy: The Tribulations of Southern Africa.*

Brian Baughan is a writer and editor who lives in Philadelphia. He is the author of *Human Rights in Africa,* also published by Mason Crest Publishers, and served as contributing editor to two study guides in Howard Bloom's MAJOR SHORT STORY WRITERS series.